Calming ANGER

Bee Social Prep Stories

PUBLISHER'S NOTE: This is a work of fiction. Names, characters, places and incidents are either the product of the author's imagination or are used fictitiously, and any resemblance to actual persons, living or dead, business establishments, schools, events, or locales is entirely coincidental.

ISBN: 9798340652102

Calming Anger: A Social Prep Story or Anger Management And Managing Difficult Feelings and Emotions

Everyone gets angry sometimes.
It is okay to feel angry!

ANGER IS AN EMOTION JUST LIKE HAPPINESS OR SADNESS.

However, there are times when those feelings of anger can grow so intense that they feel impossible to control.

WHEN THAT HAPPENS, YOU MIGHT FIND YOURSELF YELLING, SCREAMING, OR SAYING THINGS YOU DON'T REALLY MEAN. SOMETIMES, IT CAN EVEN LEAD TO BREAKING THINGS OR HURTING YOURSELF OR THOSE AROUND YOU.

UNDERSTANDING AND MANAGING HOW ANGER AFFECTS YOU IS CRUCIAL FOR BETTER CONTROL IN DIFFICULT SITUATIONS.

STAGE 1

ANNOYED STAGE

ANGER OFTEN BEGINS WITH A SENSE OF IRRITATION. YOUR MUSCLES MAY TENSE UP, YOU BECOME MORE SENSITIVE, AND YOU MIGHT FIND YOURSELF SNAPPING AT OTHERS WHEN THEY SPEAK TO YOU.

STAGE 2

FRUSTRATED STAGE

AS ANGER BUILDS, YOU MAY NOTICE YOUR BODY HEATING UP, YOUR HEART RACING, AND YOUR MIND FILLING WITH FURIOUS THOUGHTS.

STAGE 3

ENRAGED STAGE

AS ANGER INTENSIFIES, IT CAN BECOME HARDER TO STAY IN CONTROL. YOU MIGHT ACT IN WAYS YOU NORMALLY WOULDN'T, LIKE YELLING, CRYING, OR STOMPING YOUR FEET.

STAGE 4

OUT-OF-CONTROL STAGE

THIS IS THE PEAK OF ANGER, WHERE CONTROL SLIPS AWAY. YOU MIGHT FIND YOURSELF LASHING OUT—THROWING OR KICKING THINGS, BREAKING OBJECTS, OR USING EXCESSIVE SWEARING. IN EXTREME CASES, IT CAN LEAD TO THREATS OF VIOLENCE OR EVEN SELF-HARM.

WHEN ANGER CONTROLS YOU, IT'S LIKE CARRYING A TICKING TIME BOMB, READY TO EXPLODE AT ANY MOMENT.

This can create fear and tension in those around you, making it difficult to communicate effectively. Instead of resolving issues, unchecked anger often escalates situations, leaving everyone involved feeling worse than before.

The good news is there are ways you can calm down when you get angry.

One of the best things you can do to calm down is take some deep breaths.

GIVE IT A TRY

BREATH IN THROUGH YOUR NOSE

BLOW OUT THROUGH YOUR MOUTH

You can also count to ten. This is a really great way to calm down.

4
7
10

THERE ARE ALSO ACTIVITIES YOU CAN DO THAT CAN HELP YOU RELAX AND UNWIND.

THESE ACTIVITIES ARE CALLED COPING SKILLS.

GOING FOR A WALK OR EXERCISING

DRAWING OR JOURNALING

LISTENING TO MUSIC

These activities can be anything that make you feel better.

They are like special tricks you can use when you're feeling upset, worried, or mad. When you use these tricks, it's like telling your brain, "Hey, it's okay, I've got this!"

SQUEEZING A SQUISHY TOY
PLAYING WITH SLIME
SINGING AND DANCING
BLOWING BUBBLES
PLAYING WITH A FIDGET SPINNER

ANGRY
BUTTON

LEARN WHAT PUSHES YOUR ANGRY BUTTON?

UNDERSTANDING WHAT TRIGGERS YOUR ANGER IS CRUCIAL FOR MANAGING EMOTIONS EFFECTIVELY. THE MOST COMMON CAUSES OF ANGER ARE:

FRUSTRATION

STRUGGLING WITH NEW OR DIFFICULT TASKS CAN LEAD TO FRUSTRATION AND ANGER.

FEELING UNHEARD

WHEN YOU ARE IGNORED OR NOT ACKNOWLEDGED YOU CAN BECOME FRUSTRATED AND ANGRY.

CONFLICTS

PROBLEMS WITH FRIENDS, BULLYING, OR EXCLUSION CAN EVOKE ANGER.

THINGS NOT GOING AS PLANNED

IT CAN BE FRUSTRATING WHEN THINGS DON'T GO AS PLANNED.

BEING CRITICIZED

HARSH CRITICISM CAN LEAD TO FEELINGS OF ANGER.

PHYSICAL DISCOMFORT

BEING HUNGRY OR TIRED CAN TRIGGER ANGER.

UNFAIR TREATMENT

FEELING THAT YOU ARE BEING TREATED UNFAIRLY CAN BE A MAJOR TRIGGER.

WATCH OUT FOR ANGRY THOUGHTS.

IT'S EASY TO GET STUCK IN A GRUMPY MOOD WHEN ANGRY THOUGHTS GET STUCK IN YOUR HEAD. WHEN THAT HAPPENS YOU NEED TO FLIP THOSE THOUGHTS AROUND WITH SOME POSITIVE THINKING!

BUILD YOUR 'NO-MEANIES' ZONE!"

YOU DESERVE TO BE TREATED WITH KINDNESS! LEARN HOW TO SET UP YOUR OWN 'NO-MEANIES' ZONE AND KEEP THOSE WHO ARE MEAN AND BULLY YOU FAR, FAR AWAY.

TALKING HELPS.

WHEN ANGER FEELS TOO BIG TO HANDLE, SHARING IT WITH A TRUSTED ADULT CAN HELP LIGHTEN THE LOAD AND FIND SOLUTIONS.

When Therapy Might Be Required

Anger is a natural and healthy emotion that children experience as they grow and face new challenges. During different developmental stages, kids often use anger to express feelings of frustration, confusion, or distress when they struggle to communicate their needs or manage overwhelming emotions. This is a normal part of learning how to navigate the world. However, when a child's anger becomes frequent, intense, or increasingly unmanageable—such as when it escalates into physical aggression, tantrums, self-harm, or destructive behavior—it may signal deeper underlying issues like anxiety, depression, trauma, or difficulties with emotional regulation. In these cases, professional intervention might be necessary to prevent long-term emotional and behavioral problems. Recognizing these signs early can help address the root causes before they become more ingrained and harder to manage.

Persistent Outbursts

Occasional outbursts are a normal part of childhood, especially during certain developmental stages, such as toddlerhood and adolescence. However, if a child displays frequent, severe, or escalating episodes of anger that disrupt daily functioning or lead to physical aggression, self-harm, or harm to others, it could be a sign that deeper issues need to be addressed. In such cases, therapy can help identify the underlying causes of anger and provide the child with healthier coping mechanisms.

Impact on Relationships

When anger begins to strain a child's relationships with family members, peers, or teachers, it can lead to social isolation, rejection, or bullying. If a child struggles to make or keep friends, often argues with authority figures, or withdraws from social interactions due to their anger, therapy can offer them the skills needed to navigate social situations more effectively.

Emotional and Behavioral Issues

Anger in children can sometimes be a symptom of emotional disorders such as anxiety, depression, Oppositional Defiant Disorder (ODD), or Attention-Deficit/Hyperactivity Disorder (ADHD). If a child exhibits signs of excessive worry, sadness, hyperactivity, defiance, or impulsivity alongside anger, therapy can play a crucial role in managing both the anger and its root causes.

Difficulty Expressing Emotions

Some children may not have the language or self-awareness to articulate their feelings, leading to frustration and anger. If a child consistently reacts with anger because they find it challenging to express other emotions like sadness, fear, or disappointment, therapy can provide them with emotional literacy and tools to better identify and communicate their feelings.

Academic Performance

Persistent anger can affect a child's ability to concentrate, follow instructions, or participate in school activities, leading to declining academic performance. When a child's anger interferes with their learning or disrupts the classroom environment, therapy can help address the root of these behavioral challenges.

Physical Symptoms

When a child's anger begins to manifest as physical symptoms, such as frequent headaches, stomachaches, or sleep disturbances, it may be a sign that they are struggling to process their emotions effectively. These physical symptoms can occur because the body often reacts to intense stress and unresolved anger. For instance, chronic tension from anger can lead to muscle aches, while constant worry can disrupt sleep patterns. If a child consistently complains of these symptoms without a clear medical cause, therapy might be necessary to address the emotional turmoil.

WHAT KIND OF THERAPY WORKS BEST?

Several therapeutic approaches have proven effective in helping children manage their anger, with some focusing on changing thought patterns and behaviors, while others emphasize emotional regulation and social skills. The choice of therapy often depends on the child's age, specific needs, and the underlying causes of their anger.

COGNITIVE-BEHAVIORAL THERAPY

CBT is one of the most widely used and effective therapies for managing anger in children. This approach focuses on identifying and altering negative thought patterns that lead to anger. It teaches children to recognize the triggers of their anger, understand the connection between their thoughts, emotions, and behaviors, and develop coping strategies to manage their responses.

Why CBT Works: CBT is practical and goal-oriented, providing children with specific tools they can use to handle anger-inducing situations. For example, it might involve teaching a child to use deep breathing, positive self-talk, or a 'stop and think' technique before reacting.

PLAY THERAPY

Play therapy is particularly effective for younger children who may not yet have the verbal skills to express their thoughts and emotions. Through play, therapists can observe a child's behaviors, identify underlying issues contributing to their anger, and help the child explore and express their feelings in a safe, non-threatening manner.

Why Play Therapy Works: Play therapy allows children to act out scenarios and emotions they might not be able to articulate otherwise. The therapist can use toys, games, and storytelling to help children understand their emotions and learn healthier ways to cope with anger.

FAMILY THERAPY

Sometimes a child's anger is rooted in family dynamics, such as communication problems, inconsistent discipline, or high levels of stress within the home. Family therapy involves working with the child and their family members to improve interactions, set healthy boundaries, and create a more supportive home environment.

Why Family Therapy Works: Addressing anger in a family context helps everyone involved understand their role in the child's emotional well-being.

DIALECTICAL BEHAVIOR THERAPY

DBT, a form of CBT, is often used for older children and adolescents who experience intense emotions. DBT focuses on teaching skills in emotional regulation, distress tolerance, mindfulness, and interpersonal effectiveness. These skills can help manage anger in a healthy and controlled manner.

Why DBT Works: DBT provides children with concrete strategies for handling overwhelming emotions. Through mindfulness practices, they learn to become more aware of their feelings and responses, allowing them to intervene in their anger cycle before it escalates.

SOCIAL SKILLS TRAINING

For some children, anger issues stem from difficulties in social interactions, such as not knowing how to express feelings, handle conflicts, or interpret social cues. Social skills training helps children learn effective communication, problem-solving, and conflict-resolution techniques.

Why Social Skills Training Works: By teaching children how to interact positively with others, they can reduce frustration and misunderstandings that often lead to anger. Improved social skills help them build better relationships, increasing their confidence and reducing the likelihood of angry outbursts during social interactions.

WHEN I CONTROL
MY ANGER, I FEEL
PROUD OF MYSELF.

Made in the USA
Las Vegas, NV
29 December 2024